THE Outback

ANNALIESE PORTER

Illustrated by

BRONWYN BANCROFT

Magabala Books

Dark, red earth

surrounding flat, stony plains—

gibbers lay on scorching sand,

where seldom it rains.

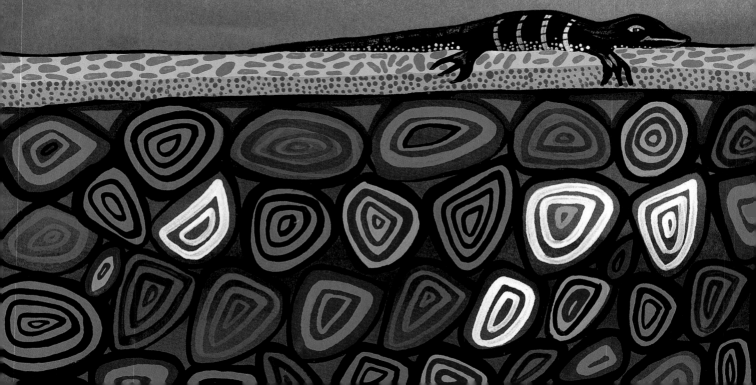

A desert interior—

harsh, sandy, miles of dunes,

the scurrying of animals

are the only tunes.

Scaly snakes and lizards,
dingoes, wombats, kangaroos,
numbats, tiny bugs,
and flocks of cockatoos.

Yes, there's more to the Outback
than vast plains and parched earth—
lots of animals need shelter here,
from Muttaburra to east of Perth.

There are flowering wattle,

desert lime and pea,

beneath the ivory clouds—

home to the spinifex and gidgee.

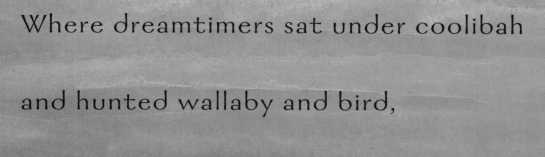

Where dreamtimers sat under coolibah

and hunted wallaby and bird,

the Outback is sacred—

a place where the didgeridoo is heard.

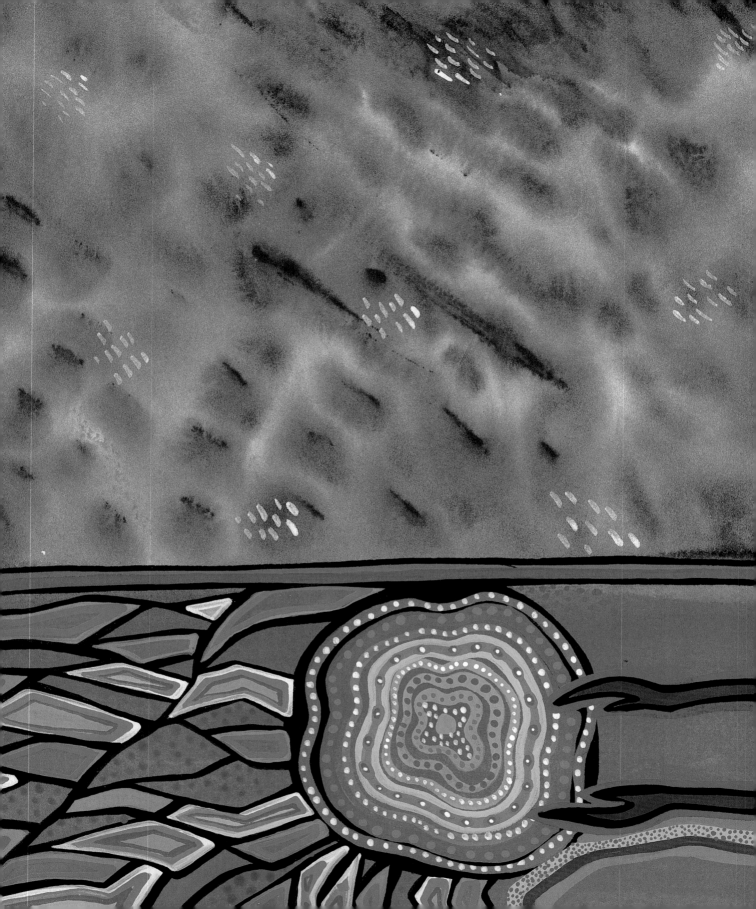

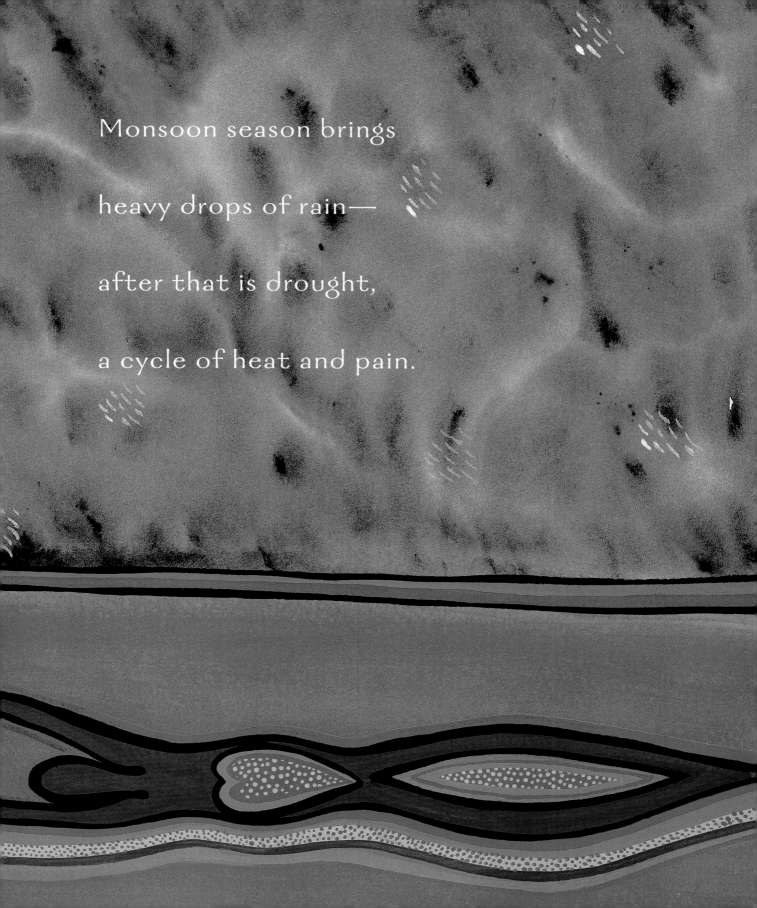

Monsoon season brings

heavy drops of rain—

after that is drought,

a cycle of heat and pain.

On Uluru there are many shades

on the rocky eye—

browns and reds mingling

into a rich earthy dye.

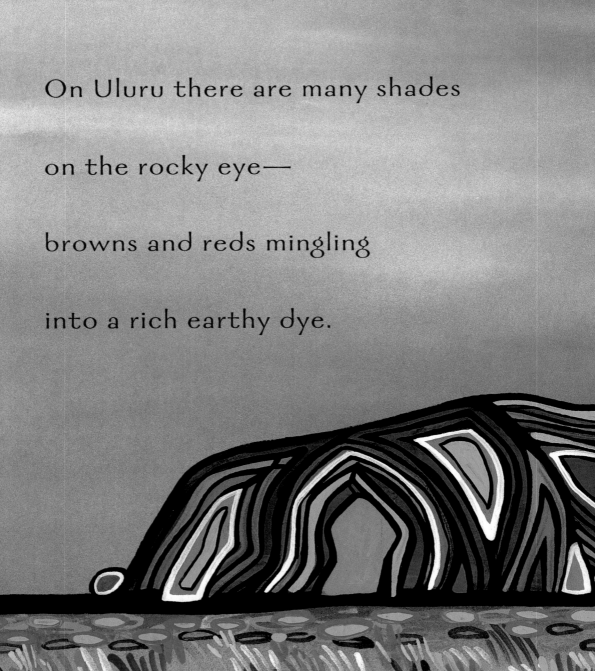

Sky blues and yellows,

red, green and white—

the rainbow of colours

create a radiant sight.

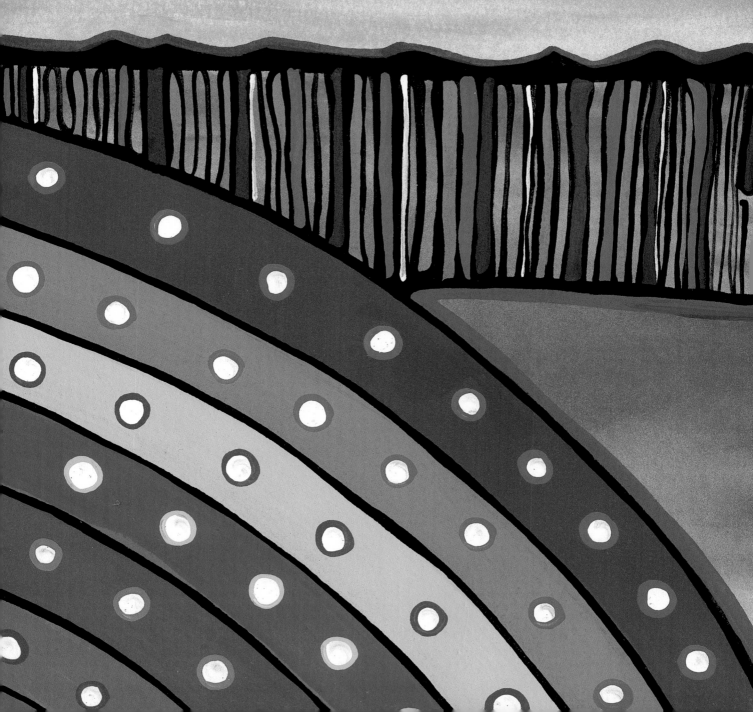

Ancient dreaming stories,
paintings drawn on rock
by the hunters of the kookaburra—
tracked by its cry of mock.

We feel this hallowed place

and know the Outback's awesome light,

where the dingo's howl is endless—

where the galahs take to flight.

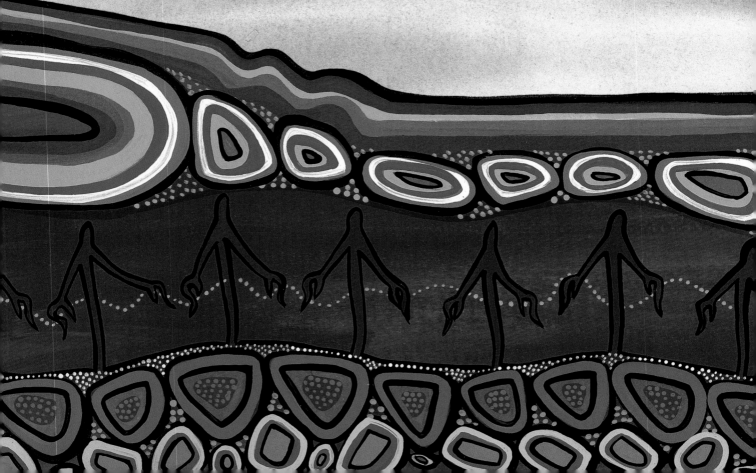

For thousands of years Aboriginal people
have trodden on this dusty sand—
caring for mother nature
and their sacred land.

They have felt the softness of country
and seen the crystal sky—
they have tasted the searing desert wind
and heard the eagle's cry.

First published in 2005, published in paperback 2008, reprinted 2009, 2012, 2014, 2015
Magabala Books Aboriginal Corporation, Broome, Western Australia
Website: www.magabala.com   Email: orders@magabala.com

Magabala Books receives financial assistance from the Commonwealth Government through the
Australia Council, its arts advisory body. The State of Western Australia has made an investment in
this project through the Department of Culture and the Arts in association with Lotterywest.

Designed by Pigs Might Fly Productions
Typeset in 22 pt Galahad
Printed in China by Everbest Printing Company Ltd

National Library of Australia
Cataloguing-in-Publication data:

Porter, Annaliese, 1993- .
The outback/Annaliese Porter; Illustrated by Bronwyn Bancroft

New ed.
For children.
ISBN 9781921248047 (pbk).

1. Aboriginal Australians, Juvenile fiction.
2. Picture books for children - Australia
Bancroft, Bronwyn.

A823.4

Australian Government

Australia Council for the Arts

Government of Western Australia
Department of Culture and the Arts

lotterywest
supported

About the illustrator

Bronwyn Bancroft is a descendant of the Bundjalung people of New South Wales and, over the past 30 years, has undertaken public art commissions, imagery design for private commission and authoring and illustrating children's books. First and foremost, however, Bronwyn creates her own signature style of contemporary artwork which continues to be exhibited nationally and internationally. Bronwyn is passionately involved in the pursuit of advancing Aboriginal Health and Education as well as protecting the rights of Aboriginal people. She currently serves on the boards of Boomalli Aboriginal Artists Co-operative, the Copyright Agency and the Australian Indigenous Mentoring Experience (AIME). Bronwyn really enjoyed working on this book with such a young writer.

Photograph by Sharon Hickey

About the author

At only eleven years old, Annaliese Porter, is one of Australia's youngest published writers. She has been writing ever since she can remember and has received numerous awards for academic excellence and creative writing in her home state of New South Wales.

She enjoys writing short stories and poems and is currently working on her first novel…a very different kind of fairy story.

Annaliese lives in Tamworth with her family and is a descendant of the Gamilaraay people. *The Outback* is her first book.